A Marvelous Event

by Susan McCloskey

illustrations by
Tadeusz Majewski

MODERN CURRICULUM PRESS

Pearson Learning Group

The life of Don Roberto de Carlero had been more amazing than almost anyone else's in Spain. Yes, he was the same Don Roberto who, being both wealthy and generous, was known and praised all over Andalucía. He was the same Don Roberto whose vast estate grew the finest oranges, the sweetest figs, and the juiciest grapes in all Spain.

And now the great and magnificent Don Roberto was very sick. The crisis in Don Roberto's health surprised his family. To be sure, he was eighty-eight years old. But his father had lived to be 120. At least, that's what my uncle told me. When I asked for proof of this great age, my uncle said that such records were kept in an old church. Unfortunately, years earlier someone had left a candle burning in the church. This careless act resulted in a fire that burned the church to the ground.

"But why do you need proof?" my uncle asked. "For haven't I myself told you? And do I not come from the same town as Don Roberto? Surely you know that the residents of the town love the truth and never lie."

Until his sickness, Don Roberto had seemed quite healthy. Oh, he had a few of the complaints of old age—an ache here, a pain there. But while none of these ailments seemed life-threatening, his daughter became frightened one morning when she went to awaken him, and found she could not. Elena tried everything to wake her dear father. She called to him. She sprinkled water on his face. But Don Roberto did not move.

Other members of Don Roberto's family—his wife, their three sons, their two daughters, and their many grandchildren—also tried to awaken him. But Don Roberto remained as still and silent as a stone.

Don Roberto's family called for Don Julio, the doctor. Don Julio felt Don Roberto's wrist and found that his heartbeat was slow. He listened to Don Roberto's chest and found that his breathing was shallow. So he bowed his head and solemnly told Don Roberto's family that things did not look good for their beloved relative.

Don Roberto's wife, children, and grandchildren wept with sadness. They could not believe what the doctor had said. And yet they had to believe it as they saw Don Roberto lie in bed with his eyes closed. Then, Don Roberto's wife asked the servants to prepare food. She had decided to invite Don Roberto's friends and relatives to gather around him for one last time.

The servants began cooking at once. They worked all the day and into the night. Soon the tables were filled with wonderful food of all kinds.

The visitors began arriving at mid-morning the next day. After refreshing themselves with cool drinks and delicious pastries, they brushed the crumbs from their clothing and seated themselves around the bed of their dear friend and relative.

For a while, each was content with thinking his or her own thoughts. Then, as it happens at such events, they began to speak of Don Roberto, whose sickness had brought them together.

"I remember," said Don Tomás, brushing a crumb from his long mustache, "how much my dear friend Don Roberto loved horses. Especially fast horses! They say that his horse Soldado was so fast that it took three people to see him when he ran: One to say, 'Here he comes,' another to say, 'Here he is,' and a third to say, 'There he goes!' Now, I must say that I myself never saw Soldado run. However, his speed was described to me by someone from our town. And as everyone knows, our townspeople are known all over Spain for loving the truth and never lying."

The other visitors nodded. For such was the reputation of their townspeople, and they were very proud of it.

Doña Estrella spoke next.

"Don Tomás's speech reminds me of a story about our generous friend, Don Roberto," she said. "One fine day my husband and I wanted to go out to the country. However, our horse had a sore leg. So Don Roberto generously lent us Soldado. My husband harnessed Soldado to our carriage, and off we went. After we had driven a couple of miles, a ferocious wind came up. We decided to turn back.

"However, we soon found that the road was blocked by a huge oak tree that the wind had blown down. We could go nowhere. My husband refused to leave me alone while he went for help. So we waited for help to come to us.

"When we did not return home, Don Roberto became worried—as much for Soldado as for us, I dare say! He saddled a horse and set out to look for us. He found us just before dark.

"My husband suggested that Don Roberto ride to the nearest town and return with twenty strong men and two teams of oxen. These, he believed, would be necessary to move such a huge tree.

"Don Roberto smiled and said that such help was not necessary. He then walked around, examining our situation from every angle. As he walked, he muttered to himself, although I did not catch what he said. Finally, he picked up the giant oak with his bare hands. As we watched, he threw it a good distance from the road. Naturally, my husband and I were astonished at such great strength.

"When we were once again on our way, I asked Don Roberto what he had been saying to himself. He told me that he had been discussing with himself what to do. Should he move the tree aside? Or should he jump over it with my husband, me, Soldado, and the carriage in his arms? For Soldado's sake he decided to move the tree. Horses, Don Roberto explained, become frightened when all four of their feet are off the ground. He had discovered this fact as a boy when he had lifted a horse over a fence that was too high for it to jump."

Doña Estrella went on, "Now, I am sure that no one here doubts my story. After all, we in this town love the truth and never lie. However, I once told this story to some people who did not know our reputation. I am sorry to say that one of them did not believe me. I heard her say under her breath, 'Did you ever hear such foolishness?' I answered, 'Foolishness, did you say?' Then I showed her proof of my story. It was an acorn from the very oak that Don Roberto threw off the road. I keep it in the top drawer of a dresser in my bedroom. If it hasn't been lost, it is there still, for anyone who doubts the story to see."

Don Edgar then said, "To be sure, my cousin Don Roberto was the strongest man for miles around. Why, even as a young boy he was famous for his great strength. I remember a contest between him and a friend of his. Each one tried to prove that he was stronger than the other. The contest ended when Don Roberto took hold of the back of his own coat collar and lifted himself three feet off the ground. But didn't he get a scolding from his mother when he arrived home with a torn collar!"

"I myself know where he got that great strength of his," said Don Roberto's brother, Don Felipe. "I saw it with my own eyes and promised my dear brother that I would not reveal it. But now perhaps he will not mind if I share his secret."

The visitors uttered words of encouragement, and Don Felipe continued.

"One summer morning I was walking down the little road that leads to the pond. It was a hot day, and I planned to take a swim. You'll remember that there is a large pile of rocks just past a curve in that road. As I rounded the curve I came upon my brother. He was picking up a rock the size of a fist. As I opened my mouth to speak to him, he cracked the rock against a boulder as if it were an egg. Then he held the rock over his mouth and squeezed liquid out of it, drop by drop.

"My brother heard my gasp of amazement. Realizing that I had seen him, he told me that his great strength came from rock juice, which he got in the way I have just described.

"I never spoke of this before now. But like Doña Estrella, I kept proof of what I saw. For before we walked on, I picked up part of the rock that my brother cracked open for its juice. I even touched my tongue to it while it was still wet. I can tell you that rock juice tastes somewhat like lemonade.

"Alas, the rock is gone now. My daughter, not knowing any better, threw it at some rascals who were taking oranges from our trees. It has never been found."

The visitors next heard of Don Roberto's great skill as an artist.

Doña María, a favorite cousin of Don Roberto, told this story:

"As everyone knows, from the gardens of my cousin's estate come the finest grapes, figs, and oranges in all Andalucía, and maybe even all of Spain. One day my cousin arranged a bowl of these fruits. Then he began to paint them. He was determined to make the painting look as real as life.

"He left the painting for a short time to see some friends. When he returned, he surprised a few crows. They had flown in an open window and were trying to steal some fruit from the painting—the rascals!

"A servant who saw this said to Don Roberto, 'Sir, the crows have judged the worth of your painting. For in trying to snatch the fruit, they show how real you have made it seem!'

"Don Roberto, however, was not satisfied. He kept working on his painting. Finally, he put down his brush, sat down, and waited. Soon a crow flew in the window. It approached the painting and stretched out its neck. Then, as Don Roberto watched, it plucked a fig from the painting and flew off with it in its beak.

"Don Roberto said, 'Now I am satisfied. For the fruit I have painted looks so real that it has stepped into the world of being real.'"

To their surprise, the visitors next heard a familiar voice that had not spoken before now. It belonged to the man whose life they had come to praise—Don Roberto himself.

Don Roberto cleared his throat and said, "My dear family and friends, I feel as if I am waking up from a deep and dreamless sleep. I could not help but awaken when I heard Doña María's story. Please listen to me carefully.

"As you know, the people from our town love the truth and never lie. But in telling her story, Doña María said something that was not true, although I am sure she did not mean to do so."

The visitors gave Don Roberto their full attention. He continued, "Doña María's story was correct in all details except one. For the fruit that the crow plucked from my painting was not a fig. It was a grape. Everyone knows that crows love grapes more than figs, although they do eat both.

"As for the painting, I no longer have it. Here is why. One day a gentleman visited my home. He was the guest of a friend. I forget just who he was. Seeing the painting, he asked about the missing grape. My explanation fascinated him. As it turned out, he was the director of a large museum. He begged me to give the painting to his collection, and I did. Alas, I forget which museum it was. I am an old man and cannot remember everything."

Don Roberto yawned and stretched. It seemed that he was about to lie down again. Then his good friend Don Tomás said, "Don Roberto, let us all thank Doña María for the flaw in her story. For without it, you would not have awakened to correct her. You have shown that your love for the truth is so strong that nothing can conquer it.

"But now that you are awake, we beg you to stay with us. For the evening is young, and there are more stories to be told. And who knows them better than you? Please, stay!"

The visitors said many similar kind words, and finally Don Roberto agreed to stay.

I must confess that I myself did not see the marvelous event that I have described to you. It was told to me by my uncle, who was among the visitors. As I said earlier, my uncle came from the same town as Don Roberto, where they love the truth and never lie.

For any who need further proof, I can show a pastry that my uncle saved from that day. I wrapped it in a napkin and put it in a cupboard. If the mice haven't eaten it, it is there still. Shall I go look for it?